Shopping

Gill Tanner and Tim Wood

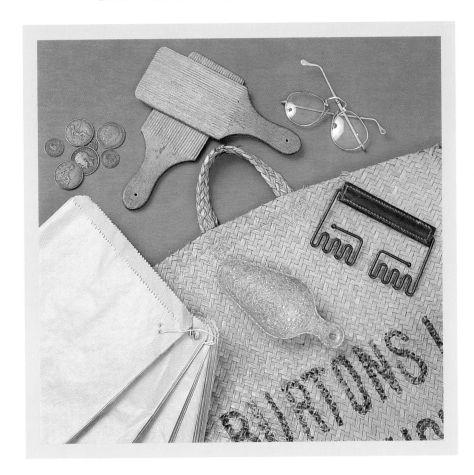

Photographs by Maggie Murray

Illustrations by Pat Tourret

A & C Black · London

Here are some of the people you will meet in this book.

The Hart family in 1990

The Cook family in 1960

Bill Hart

Linda Hart

Kerry

Lee

David Cook

June Coo[k]

Susan

Linda

Andrew

Lee Hart is the same age as you.
His sister Kerry is eight years old.
What is Lee's mum called?

This is Lee's mum Linda when she
was just nine years old in 1960.
She is with her mum and dad,
her brother and her baby sister.

The Smith family in 1930

Richard Smith

Lucy Smith

May

Jack and June

The Barker family in 1900

Charles Barker

Alice Barker

Fred

Harry

Lucy

Amy and Adam

This is Lee's granny June,
when she was just a baby in 1930.
Her brother Jack is looking after her.

This is Lee's great grandma Lucy,
when she was six years old in 1900.
Can you see what her sister and her
brothers are called?

3

Can you spot the differences between these two photographs?

One shows a modern shop
and one shows a shop one hundred
years ago.

This book is about shops and shopping.
It will help you find out how shops
and shopping have changed
in the last hundred years.

There are nine mystery objects in this book
and you can find out what they are.
They will tell you a lot about people in the past.

In 1900, every grocer used these.
They are made of wood.
They are a bit bigger than they are shown
in this picture.
They were always used together.
What do you think they were for?

Turn the page to find out.

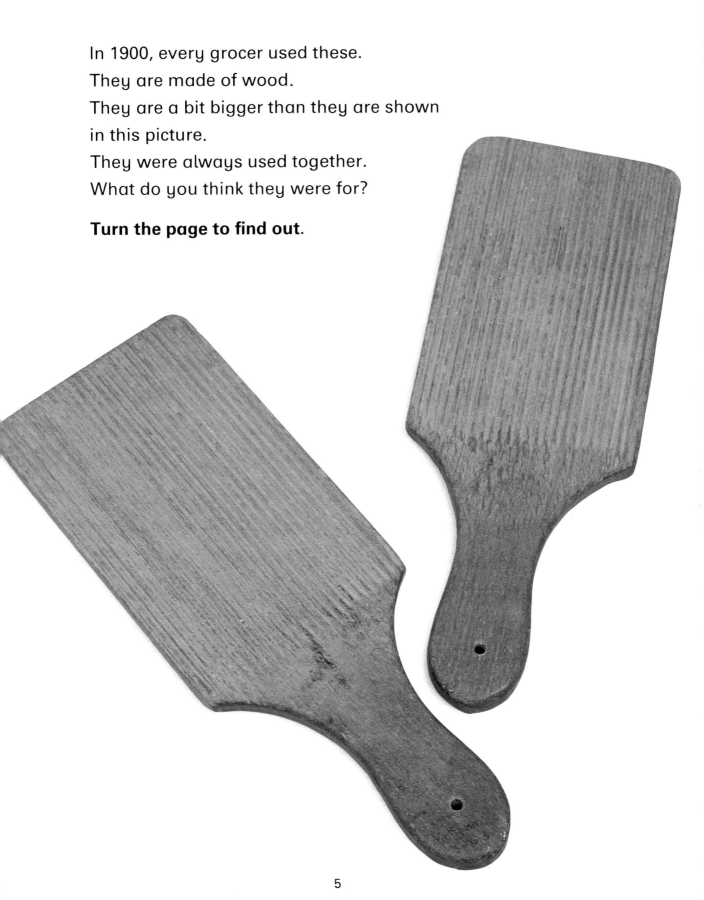

Alice Barker is shopping at the grocer's.
In those days people could buy
most of their food at the grocer's
except for fish, meat and vegetables.
Can you find the mystery objects in the picture?
They are wooden **butter-pats**.

In 1900, not many things were sold in packets.
Butter came in a big block.
The grocer cut a piece off the block and weighed it.
He patted it into shape with the butter-pats
and wrapped it in greaseproof paper.

6

This object is about the same size
as it is shown on the page.
It is made of metal and covered with cloth.
It has a chain with a clip on it.
Alice Barker used it to keep something safe.
Can you guess what?

Turn the page to find out.

Alice Barker is in the chemist's shop.
She is buying a pair of glasses.
In 1900, many people could not afford
to have proper eye tests at an optician's.
They tried on different glasses at the chemist's shop
and bought the ones which helped them to see better.
Can you spot the mystery object?
It's a **glasses case**.

In those days there was no plastic.
The lenses were made of real glass
and broke easily.
Glasses were carried in cases
to keep them safe.
This case has a hook and chain
so Alice could fasten it to her belt.

8

These mystery objects
were all used by Charles Barker.
He wore them when he went out to work.
He used two of the smaller objects
to fasten the larger object to something.

Turn the page to find out what they are.

Alice Barker and her children
are in the draper's shop.
They are choosing birthday presents for father
People went to the draper's
to buy clothes and material.
Can you spot the mystery objects?
They are a **collar** and **collar studs**.

In those days men's shirts and collars
were sold separately.
Most collars were made of white cotton material.
They were starched to make them stiff.
The collar was fixed to a shirt using two studs –
a small one at the back and a larger one at the front.

10

May would have seen this object
at the grocer's shop in 1930.
It is made of china so it is easy to wash.
The top part is about the same size
as a fruit bowl.
What do you think it was used for?

Turn the page to find out.

Lucy Smith and the children
are in the grocer's shop.
Can you spot the mystery object?
It's a **ham stand**.

In 1930, there was no plastic packaging to pre-pack food in.
Grocers who wanted to sell ham had to cook their own.
The cooked ham had a big bone in it,
so the meat had to be cut off with a sharp knife.
The grocer put the ham on a stand to make it easier to carve.

In 1930, May and Jack would have seen this object
in a sweet shop.
It's a bit bigger than your hand.
It's made of bakelite
which was rather like plastic.
What do you think it was for?

Turn the page to find out.

May and Jack are in the sweet shop
buying some aniseed balls.
In those days not many sweets
were sold in packets.
They were stored on shelves
in big glass jars.
Can you spot the mystery object?
It's a **scoop**.

Scoops were useful for serving loose,
dry food such as sweets.
The shopkeeper used the scoop
to take sweets from the jar.
She weighed the sweets on a pair of scales
Then she put them into a paper bag.

You probably know what this object is.
But do you know why it has a box on the front?
What has this object to do with shopping?
Look carefully. You might spot a big clue.

Turn the page to find out.

The butcher's boy is delivering meat
to Lucy Smith's house.
Can you see the mystery object?
It is a **delivery bike**.

In those days there were no freezers.
People had to shop for fresh food nearly every day.
Carrying heavy shopping bags was hard work
so people asked shopkeepers
to deliver the shopping to their homes.
The delivery boy put the goods
in a box or basket on the front of his bike.
He cycled round the town delivering the goods.

In 1960, the Cook family would have seen
something like this in lots of different shops.
Your arms might just be long enough to reach around it.
But you could not lift it because it is very heavy.
Does it look similar to something you see in shops today?
What do you think the keys at the front are for?

Turn the page to find out.

In the 1960s, frozen food was not as common as it is today.
Mrs Cook bought fresh fish from the fishmonger.
Can you spot the mystery object?
It's a **cash register**.

The fish were laid out on a big marble slab
which kept them cool and fresh.
First the fishmonger cut the bones out of the fish.
Then he cut up the fish and wrapped it in paper.
The fishmonger pressed keys on the cash register
to add up the bill and show the total.
A drawer in the bottom opened
so he could put the money in.

This mystery object
is about half the size of this book.
It belonged to June Cook.
Can you guess how it helped with the shopping?
Look closely, you may find a big clue.

Turn the page to find the answer.

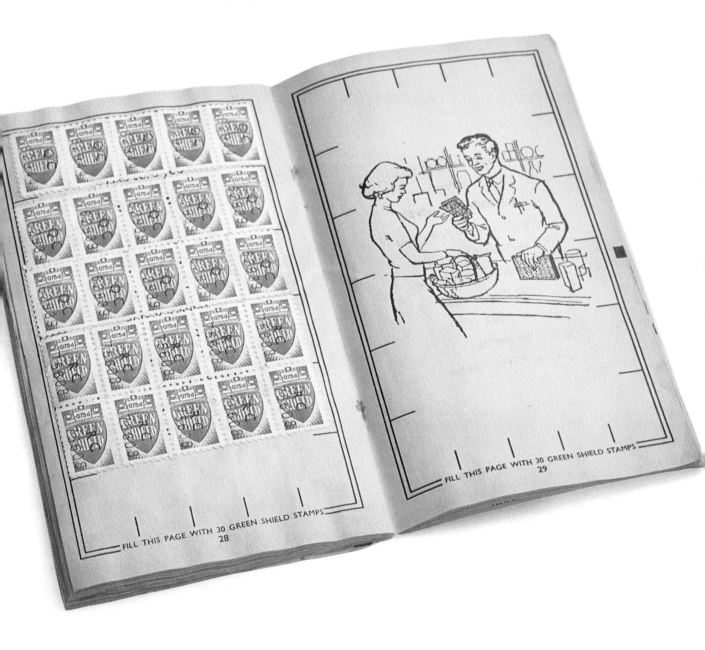

The Cooks are shopping at the supermarket.
How is it different from other shops in this book?
Can you see the mystery object?
It's a book of **trading stamps**.
The supermarket gave trading stamps to shoppers
June Cook saved up the stamps to get free gifts.

The Cooks went to the supermarket in their car
They bought enough food to last a week.
Supermarkets were a new idea in 1960.
People liked them because they could buy
most of their food in one place
instead of going to lots of different shops.

Now that you know a bit more about shops and shopping
and how they have changed over the last hundred years,
see if you can guess what these mystery objects are.

They are rolls of sticky paper
which were used to catch something.
They were mainly found in food shops.
All the children in this book saw them
and you can still buy them today.

You will find the answer on page 24.

Time-Line

These pages show you the objects in this book and the
objects which we find in shops nowadays.

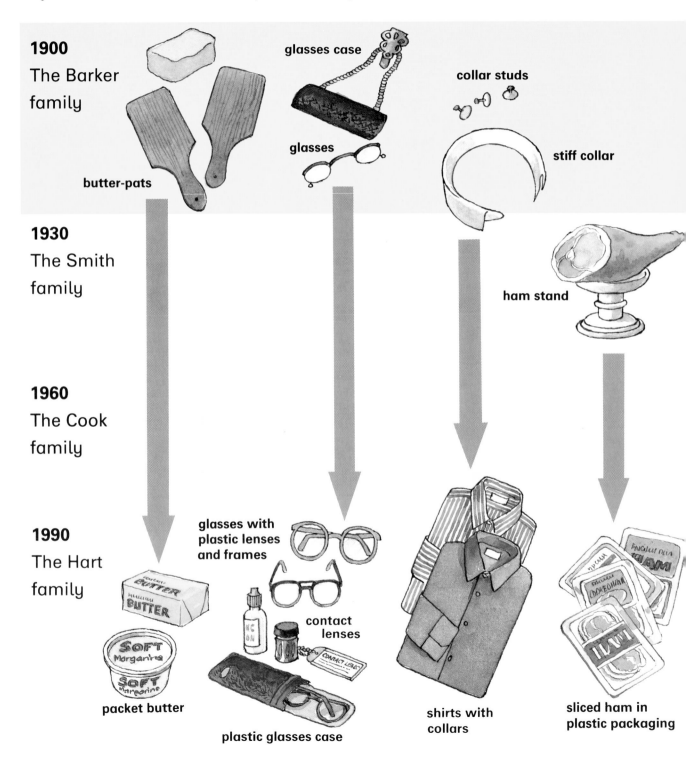

1900
The Barker
family

glasses case

collar studs

glasses

stiff collar

butter-pats

1930
The Smith
family

ham stand

1960
The Cook
family

1990
The Hart
family

glasses with
plastic lenses
and frames

contact
lenses

BUTTER

SOFT
Margarine

SOFT
Margarine

CONTACT LENSES

packet butter

plastic glasses case

shirts with
collars

sliced ham in
plastic packaging

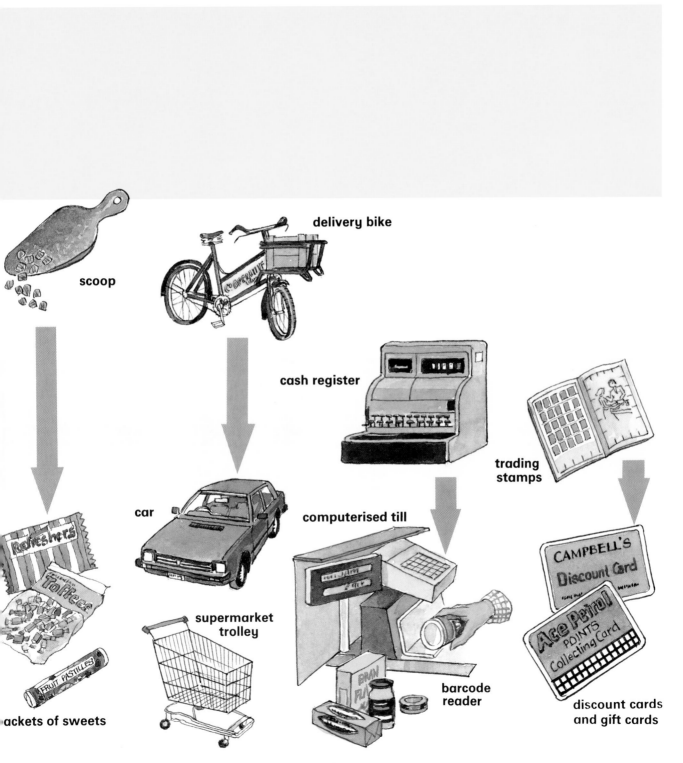

scoop

delivery bike

cash register

trading stamps

car

computerised till

Refreshers

Toffees

FRUIT PASTILLES

packets of sweets

supermarket trolley

barcode reader

CAMPBELL'S Discount Card

Ace Petrol POINTS Collecting Card

discount cards and gift cards

Index

The **mystery objects** on page 21 are **fly papers** used in shops since Lucy Barker was a child in 1900. The fly papers were unrolled and hung from the ceiling in food shops. Any flies which landed on a fly paper became stuck on the sticky surface.

For parents and teachers

More about the objects and pictures in this book

Pages 5/6 The Barker family lived in a large industrial town. Shopping in 1900 meant visiting street sellers, markets and specialist shops which offered a personal service. Pre-packaged food was uncommon and fresh produce was hard to find.

Pages 7/8 There were a few specialist optician's shops in 1900 but most people bought glasses 'off the shelf' at the chemist. Those who could afford to go to the optician went through the simplest of eye tests.

Pages 9/10 Only major department stores sold 'off the peg' clothes. Rich people had their clothes made. Others made their own or bought them secondhand. Stiff collars were changed every day so a shirt could be worn for longer before it had to be washed.

Pages 11/12 The Smiths lived in a semi-detached house in a small town. Grocers sold a great number of items, such as flour and biscuits, loose. Other goods, such as cheese, were sliced off large blocks.

Pages 13/14 The earliest eating chocolate in the UK was probably Fry's Chocolate Lozenges which went on sale in 1826. Some of the sweets sold in 1930, such as bullseye and aniseed balls are still popular today.

Pages 15/16 Most food shops in the 1930s had delivery boys who delivered the same day. As the number of motor cars and supermarkets increased, the 'weekly shop' ended their importance.

Pages 17/18 The Cooks lived in one of the new towns built in the 1960s. Note the dual prices on the cash register. Decimalisation began in 1968 and was completed in 1971. Most modern cash registers are electronic.

Pages 19/20 The UK's first full-size supermarket opened in 1948. With the increasing number of cars and home freezers, it ended the need for a daily shop. The number of trading stamps given depended on the amount spent.

Things to do

History Mysteries will provide an excellent starting point for all kinds of history work. There are lots of general ideas which can be drawn out of the pictures, particularly in relation to the way shops, clothes, family size and lifestyles have changed in the last 100 years. Below are some starting points and ideas for follow up activities.

1 Work on families and family trees can be developed from the families on pages 2/3, bearing in mind that many children do not come from two-parent, nuclear families. Why do the families in the book have different surnames even though they are related? How have their clothes and hair styles changed over time?

2 Find out more about shops and shopping in the past from a variety of sources, including interviews with older people in the community, books, museums and reconstructed shops. Shopping wasn't the same for everyone. Why not?

3 There is one object which is in one picture of the 1900s, one picture of the 1930s, and one picture of the 1960s. Can you find it?

4 Make a local study of the shops near your school and/or arrange a field trip to a museum such as Buckley's Shop Museum or York Castle Museum.

5 Look at the differences between the photographs and the illustrations in this book. What different kinds of things can they tell you?

6 Make your own collection of shopping objects or pictures. You can build up an archive or school museum over several years by encouraging children to bring in old objects, collecting unwanted items from parents, collecting from junk shops and rumble sales. You may also be able to borrow handling collections from your local museum or library service.

7 Encouraging the children to look at the objects is a useful start, but they will get more out of this if you organise some practical activities which help to develop their powers of observation. These might include drawing the objects, describing an object to another child who must then pick out the object from the collection, or writing descriptions of the objects for labels or for catalogue cards.

8 Encourage the children to answer questions. What do the objects look and feel like? What are they made of? What makes them work? How old are they? How could you find out more about them? Do they do the job they are supposed to do?

9 What do the objects tell us about the people who used them? Children might do some writing, drawing or role play, imagining themselves as the owners of different objects.

10 Children might find a mystery object in their own home or school for the others to draw, write about and identify. Children can compare the objects in the book with objects in their own home or school.

11 If you have an exhibition, try pairing old objects with their nearest modern counterparts. Talk about each pair. Some useful questions might be: How can you tell which is older? Which objects have changed most over time? Why? What do you think of the older objects? What would people have thought of them when they were new? Can you test how well the objects work? Is the modern version better than the old version?

12 Make a time-line using your objects. You might find the time-line at the back of this book useful. You could include pictures in your time-line and other markers to help the children gain a sense of chronology. Use your time-line to bring out the elements of *change* (eg. the gradual development of self-service stores, supermarkets, weekly shopping by car, the disappearance of specialist shops, availability of a wider variety of goods, improved preservation and packaging techniques) and *continuity* (eg. basic need for people to buy goods and the need for shops).

History Mysteries

First published 1993
A & C Black (Publishers) Limited
35 Bedford Row, London WC1R 4JH

ISBN 0-7136-3689-0

© 1993 A & C Black (Publishers) Limited

Acknowledgements

The authors and publishers would like to thank Suella Postles and the staff of Brewhouse
Yard Museum, Nottingham; Mrs Tanner's Tangible History; Pork Farms (Nottingham);
Len Needham Greengrocer (West Bridgford, Nottingham).

Photographs by Maggie Murray except for: p4 (top) Beamish, The North of England Open
Air Museum, County Durham; p4 (bottom) Joanna O'Brien, Format Photographers.

Filmset by Rowland Phototypesetting Limited, Bury St Edmunds, Suffolk
Printed and bound in Italy by L.E.G.O.